SPARKY AND EDDIE
WILD, WILD RODEO!

SPARKY AND EDDIE
WILD, WILD RODEO!

by Tony Johnston
pictures by Susannah Ryan

Scholastic Press
New York

LIBRARY OF CONGRESS CATALOGING-IN-PUBLICATION DATA
Johnston, Tony; 1942–
Sparky and Eddie : wild, wild rodeo! / by Tony Johnston :
illustrated by Susannah Ryan.   p.   cm.
Summary: When two best friends compete in a mock
rodeo at school, they learn that winning is not everything.
ISBN 0-590-47984-9 (hc). — ISBN 0-590-47985-7 (pb).
[1. Schools — Fiction. 2. Friendship — Fiction.
3. Cowboys — Fiction.] I. Ryan, Susannah, ill. II. Title.
PZ7.J6478Sp   1997   [E]—dc20   96-38188   CIP   AC

10 9 8 7 6 5 4 3 2 1   8 9/9 0/0 01 02 03
Printed in Mexico   49
First edition, April 1998
The illustrations for this book were created using watercolors.
The text type for this book was set in Janson Text.
Design by Kristina Iulo

For Gayle and Gary Libberton
and for the kids of Black Bob School,
Olathe, Kansas — YA-HOO!
T. J.

For Polly, our cowgirl.
S. R.

Sparky and Eddie were excited.

Today was the rodeo.

It was Sparky's class against Eddie's.

Sparky wore a vest with fringe,
jeans, a string tie,
and his father's boots.
The boots were too big.
He could hardly walk.
But he didn't care.
He was a cowboy
and happy.

Eddie wore a shirt with a cow,
jeans, a red bandanna,
and his father's hat.
The hat was too big.
He could hardly see.
But he didn't care.
He was a cowboy and happy.

Sparky and Eddie galloped to school.
They galloped on sock-headed horses.
They smacked their jeans with their hands.
SMACK! SMACK! SMACK!

They carried teddy bears.
"YA-HOO!" they yelled,
all the way to school.

Their classes gathered outside.
All the kids were cowboys.
Or cowgirls.
They all had teddy bears.
They all galloped around on
sock-headed horses.
They all smacked their jeans.
SMACK! SMACK! SMACK!
They all yelled, "YA-HOO!"

"Settle down," a teacher said.

He gave them his settle-down look.

Eddie didn't settle down.

He kept galloping.

Sparky wanted the rodeo to start.
He wanted his class to win.
"Settle down," Sparky told Eddie.
He gave Eddie his settle-down look.
Eddie settled down.

The principal said, "Howdy.

Welcome to the rodeo.

We have three events.

The class with the most points wins."

Then she yelled, "YA-HOO!"

The first event was Teddy Bear Roping.

Really, it was stringing.

The kids had to run to their teddy bears,

then tie their bears' legs together

with string.

Kids set their teddy bears down.

Sparky and Eddie did that, too.

The principal called,
"*One, two, three.*
GO!"
The ropers ran to their teddy bears.

They grabbed their teddy bears.
They tossed their teddy bears down.
Then, loop, loop, loop,
they tied some legs together.
They tied fast.

They tied *so* fast,
some kids tied their fingers in
with the teddy bear legs.
Eddie tied his thumb.

Sparky's class won.

They got ten points.

"YA-HOO!" Sparky yelled.

He liked to win.

The Boot Search was next.
Kids pulled off their boots
and threw them in a pile.
The pile was Boot Hill.
Teachers mixed up the boots.
The first class to find theirs
and put them back on would win.

The principal called,
"*One, two, three.*
GO!"

The kids dashed and darted
and dug for their boots.
They screeched and screamed
and scrambled for their boots.
They hooted and scooted
and rooted for their boots.

Sparky's boots were so big,
he found them first.
His whole class found
their boots first.
They got ten points.
"YA-HOO!" yelled Sparky.
He liked to win.

The Tortilla Toss was last.
At a signal,
the teams tossed stale tortillas.
Tortillas and tortillas and tortillas.
They sailed through the air
like thin, white Frisbees.

Sparky's class was ahead.

It was Eddie's turn.

His tortilla was ready.

Eddie was ready.

But—his hat fell over his eyes.

Eddie couldn't see.

He tossed anyway.

His tortilla sailed far.

So far, his class won.

They got twenty points.

"*Pooh!*" Sparky said.

He hated to lose.

Now the points were even.

The classes were tied.

No one had won.

The principal said,

"We'll have one more event.

Whoever names the most uses

for a bandanna wins the rodeo."

"Uses for a *banana*?" the kids asked.

"Bandanna," she said.

Sparky's class huddled.

They knew about bandannas.

They yelled a bandanna list.

Their teacher wrote it—fast.

They yelled things like:

fix broken bones

cover eyes

cover mouth

wipe sweat

They yelled fifteen things
for their bandanna list.

Eddie's class huddled.

They didn't know about bandannas.

They yelled a bandanna list.

They yelled:

"WE DON'T KNOW!"

Eddie said, "Wait."

Eddie liked to know stuff.

He knew about bandannas.

He yelled a new bandanna list

for his class.

The teacher wrote it—fast.

He yelled things like:

GAG
RAG
BAG
HATBAND
DIAPER
FLAG

Eddie yelled thirty-four things
for the bandanna list.
Eddie's class won the rodeo.
"YA-HOO!" Eddie shouted.
"YA-HOO!" his class shouted.

"POOH!" Sparky shouted.
He was mad.
He was so mad,
he started to cry.
He stomped off.
He stomped off in his too-big boots
to let his tears fall—alone.

Eddie found Sparky.

Eddie felt sad.

"Sorry I knew about bandannas,"
he said.

Sparky looked at Eddie.

"You couldn't help it," Sparky said.
"You're a brain."

Then he said, "Sorry I got mad.
I'm glad you won."

"You are?" Eddie asked.

"Yes. I like you better
than I like to win.
You are my best friend."

Eddie felt happy then.

He looked at Sparky's wet face.

He smiled.

"I know one more use for a bandanna."

"What?" Sparky asked.

"To dry tears."

Eddie gave his bandanna to Sparky.

"Thanks." Sparky smiled.

Then they smacked their jeans.
SMACK! SMACK! SMACK!
And they galloped their sock-headed
horses to their rooms.
"YA-HOO!" they yelled.
For they were cowboys and happy.